Noodleheads
FIND SOMETHING FISHY

by Tedd Arnold
Martha Hamilton
and Mitch Weiss

illustrated by Tedd Arnold

Holiday House New York

In memory of Tackle Box Charlie
—T. A.

For Mollie and Alexandra, charter
members of the Noodlehead Club
—M. H. and M. W.

Text copyright © 2018 by Tedd Arnold, Martha Hamilton, and Mitch Weiss
Illustrations copyright © 2018 by Tedd Arnold
All Rights Reserved
HOLIDAY HOUSE is registered at the U.S. Patent and Trademark Office.
Printed in bound in September 2019 at Toppan Leefung, DongGuan City, China.
The artwork was rendered digitally using Photoshop software.
www.holidayhouse.com
1 3 5 7 9 10 8 6 4 2

Library of Congress Cataloging-in-Publication Data:

Names: Arnold, Tedd, author, illustrator.
Title: Noodleheads find something fishy / by Tedd Arnold, Martha Hamilton, and Mitch Weiss ;
illustrated by Tedd Arnold.
Description: First edition. | New York : Holiday House, [2018]
Summary: Brothers Mac and Mac are outwitted by Cousin Meatball, three fish, and even a fishing rod
when they set out to learn something new. Includes author's note on tales of fools and the motifs
found in this story.
Identifiers: LCCN 2017050087 | ISBN 9780823439379 (hardcover)
Subjects: LCSH: Fools and jesters—Fiction. | Fishing—Fiction. | Boats and boating—Fiction.
| Brothers—Fiction. | Humorous stories.
Classification: LCC PZ7.A7379 Nt 2018| DDC [E]—dc23
LC record available at https://lccn.loc.gov/2017050087

ISBN: 978-0-8234-4437-3 (paperback)

NOODLEHEADS
FIND SOMETHING FISHY

CHAPTER 1

HOW TO GROW A BOAT

One morning, a few weeks later, Mom had an idea for Mac and Mac.

Don't just sit inside being bored. Go outside and enjoy this beautiful day.

NOODLEHEADS
FIND SOMETHING FISHY

NOODLEHEADS FIND SOMETHING FISHY

CHAPTER 3
THE BIGGEST FISH

We went fishing. And a fish taught us that the biggest fish is **always** the one that got away.

It's **true!** We had the biggest fish, and it got away!

Authors' Notes

Story Sources for *Noodleheads Find Something Fishy*

Everyone has done something foolish at one time or another. As a result, tales of fools, also called "noodles" or "noodleheads," have been told for as long as people have told stories. In 1888, W. A. Clouston wrote a scholarly book called *The Book of Noodles* in which he described numerous stories that had been told for hundreds of years, and quite a few dating back more than two millennia. We have used these old stories as inspiration for Mac and Mac's adventures. People around the world tell similar stories about their particular fools, such as Giufà in Italy, Nasreddin Hodja in Turkey, Juan Bobo in Puerto Rico, and Jack in England. The expression "Fortune, that favors fools" is apt, for, in spite of their foolishness, things usually turn out fine in the end for the fool. Perhaps this is because they are generally kind and well-meaning. Noodlehead stories help children to understand humor and logical thinking; kids quickly see that noodleheads are totally illogical—usually to an absurd extent.

The motifs to which we refer in the information that follows are from *The Storyteller's Sourcebook: A Subject, Title, and Motif Index to Folklore Collections for Children* by Margaret Read MacDonald, 1st edition (Detroit: Gale, 1982) and 2nd edition (Detroit: Gale, 2001). Tale types are from *A Guide to Folktales in the English Language* by D. L. Ashliman (NY: Greenwood, 1987).

Introduction

The motif in this section is J2171.6.2, Potter cannot get pole through gate. In Lee Wyndham's *Tales People Tell in China* (NY: Messner, 1970, p. 64), a pottery maker, hoping to sell his pots in a nearby town, puts them in two nets, ties the nets to the ends of a bamboo pole, and carries the pole on his shoulders. He can't, however, figure out how to get the long pole through the town gate. First the potter carries the pole horizontally, and the gate is too narrow. Then he holds it vertically, and the gate is too low. A wise bystander notices and advises the potter to carry it lengthwise or sideways. In another variant found in *Sweet and Sour: Tales from China* by Carol Kendall and Yao-wen Li (NY: Seabury, 1978, pp. 45–48), the town magistrate is named Old Fuddlement because of his lack of common sense. When a fool, or "muddlehead," as a fool is called in this town, makes the same mistake as the potter, Old Fuddlement's silly advice is, "Why didn't you saw the pole in two? You could have been home in bed by now!"

Chapter 1: How to Grow a Boat

The motif in this chapter is J2212.7*, Boat expected to grow into a ship. The inspiration came from "The Little Boat" in Lillian Bason's collection *Those Foolish Molboes!* (NY: Cowan, McCann & Geoghegan, 1977). In Denmark, they tell stories of an entire village of fools who live on the peninsula of Mols and are known as the Molboes. This is Denmark's equivalent to the Jewish village of Chelm in Poland, or Gotham in England. In the story, several Molboes travel to a big city on the coast where they are impressed by one of the large ships in the harbor. They cannot afford a big ship but purchase a small one that they hope will grow in time. Alas, despite their best efforts, the little boat never becomes a big ship. The captain who sells the small boat to the Molboes takes advantage of their gullibility, as Meatball does with Mac and Mac. Noodlehead stories make children aware that they should not believe everything they hear. The expression "sounds fishy" means that something seems to be dishonest or suspicious. It originated when fishermen tried to convince customers that old fish were fresh, in spite of the smell.

Chapter 2: Finding Fish

This story was inspired by "The Foolish Fisherman" in Florence Botsford's *Picture Tales from the Italian* (Philadelphia: J. B. Lippincott, 1929, pp. 13–14). After a crew of fishermen rows all night without getting anywhere, the captain is convinced that the boat is bewitched. Someone finally notices that they are still tied to the dock. The solution of the longer rope was our own idea. Uh-oh! We are starting to think like noodleheads!

The motif of marking the boat (J1922.1, Marking the place on the boat) seems to have made its way around the world. It is tale type 1278, Marking the boat. We found many examples, including an Irish version in W. A. Clouston's *The Book of Noodles* (London: Elliot Stock, 1888, p. 99); a Danish version in Lillian Bason's *Those Foolish Molboes!* (NY: Cowan, McCann & Geoghegan, 1977, pp. 36–47); and a Chinese variant in Lee Wyndham's *Tales People Tell in China* (NY: Messner, 1970, p. 66).

Chapter 3: The Biggest Fish

The inspiration for this story came from the common motif K11.1, Race won by deception: relative helpers, where a slower animal gets relatives to station them-selves at intervals in the line of a race in order to fool a faster animal. Although a race is not involved here, the concept is the same. Among the many versions we found a German variant in Wanda Gag's *More Tales from Grimm* (NY: Coward-McCann, 1947, pp. 163–170); an English version in Walter de la Mare's *Animal Stories* (NY: Scribner, 1939, pp. 3–8); and an African American version in Harold Courlander's *Terrapin's Pot of Sense* (NY: Holt, 1957, pp. 28–30). It is also tale type 275A*, The race between the hedgehog and the hare.

When Mac and Mac high-five each other, they literally "miss the boat" and fall into the water. The expression "miss the boat" began in the time before airplanes and cars when most people traveled by boat. It is also used figuratively to mean that one has missed out on an opportunity.

The phrase "learn the ropes" originated in the days of sailing ships, before they were powered by steam or fossil fuels. A new sailor would begin by learning how to tie knots and control the ropes attached to the sails in order to help the ship catch the wind. Today, of course, "learn the ropes" is used to describe learning the basics of any job.